This book belongs to

....

....

Written by Rachel Elliot
Illustrated by Julia Seal
Edited by Catherine Ard
Designed by Nicola Moore
Production by Jonathan Wakeham
Gymnastics consultant: Carol Malone

First published by Parragon in 2011

Parragon
Queen Street House
4 Queen Street
Bath BA1 1HE, UK

ISBN 978-1-4454-5639-3

Printed in China

The Littlest Gymnast

Emily and her friends love gym club.

They go every day after school.

Emily is the
smallest gymnast
in the club.

Everyone in gym club can do something special.

Everyone except Emily.

Serena swings
beautifully on the
uneven bars.

(But Emily's little
hands can't get
a good grip.)

Alison can do back
handsprings across
the floor faster than
anyone else.

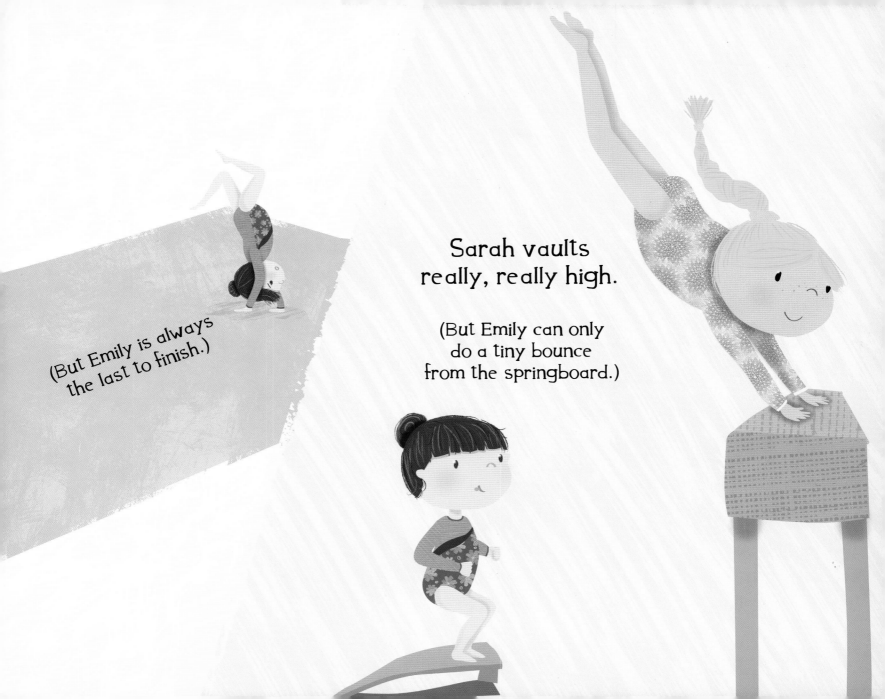

(But Emily is always the last to finish.)

Sarah vaults really, really high.

(But Emily can only do a tiny bounce from the springboard.)

Emily still loves gym club,
and she is happy for her friends.
But she wishes that she could
be best at something, too.

"I can't even balance on the beam," she thinks sadly,

as she teeters and totters.

"There's **nothing** special about **me**."

One day, their trainer, Melanie,
has some exciting news.

"Our club is taking part in a big
gymnastics display," she says.

"We **must** put on a
spectacular
show!"

Everyone has something
special to do.
Everyone except Emily.

Alison has a special floor
exercise routine with lots
of **handsprings** and **leaps**.

Serena has a complicated
routine on the uneven
bars, with difficult
moves and **twists**.

Sarah is picked to perform on the vault.

She makes it
look easy.

"There's something missing," says Melanie.
She closes her eyes and thinks hard.
"We need to finish with a big show-stopper.
I know..."

"We're going to make the **biggest** human pyramid ever!"

All of Emily's friends are in the pyramid.
It gets higher and higher.
"I just need one more gymnast to somersault
down from the very top," says Melanie.
"It needs to be someone light...

someone nimble...

It has to be the smallest
gymnast in the club."

"She . . .
means . . .
ME!"

After weeks of practice,
the day of the display
finally arrives.

Emily and her friends wait
excitedly for the events
to begin.

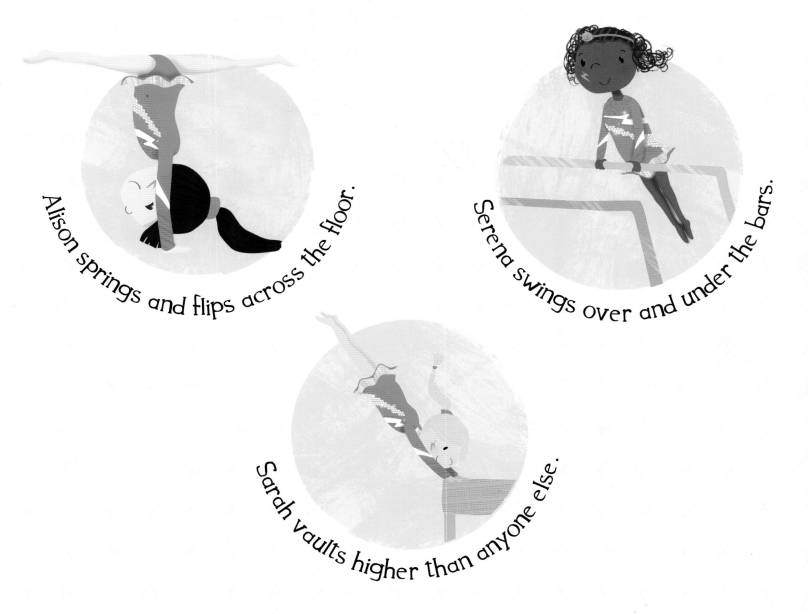

Alison springs and flips across the floor.

Serena swings over and under the bars.

Sarah vaults higher than anyone else.

Then it is time for the show-stopper . . .

The pyramid is very, very high.

Emily's legs start to **wobble** when she looks at it.

"I can do this. I can do this!" she says, bravely, and climbs into position at the very top.

Then Emily leaps into
the air and does . . .

a . . .

Perfect . . .

somersault!

She lands in the arms of the big gymnast waiting below.

"What a wonderful little gymnast," whispers the judge. Emily is given a special gymnastics necklace for her part in the display.